The Aftermeal

E D W A R D   J O N E S

Fulton Books, Inc.
Meadville, PA

First originally published by Fulton Books 2017

This book is not fiction; in fact, it is so painfully true that it hurts.
All this that we have so easily thrown away.

ISBN 978-1-63338-549-8 (Paperback)
ISBN 978-1-63338-550-4 (Digital)

Printed in the United States of America

CONTENTS

To my wife, who has made me happy again.
To my mother, who taught me how to read a book.
To my father, who was a simple man.

ACKNOWLEDGMENT

All I know is that there are two types of people in the world today: those who watch it happen and those who make it happen.

Proceeds from sale of this book would favor development of system conducive to further the longevity of life on earth.

Care. We're all in this boat together.

In loving memory of The Great Dabsy, my brother and friend.

Ashes to ashes, dust to dust, liquids to liquids, this is a must!

For more information, please see
www.theaftermealbook.com and www.omtsystems.com.

CHAPTER 1

The Problem

The Aftermeal

Trash:

1. Discarded packaging, used wrappings, after product leftover, no longer useful presentation items.
2. Foolish or pointless ideas, talk, or writing: nonsense.

Garbage:

1. Discarded contaminated trash matter (i.e., liquids, soda, paper, animal and vegetable matter, as from a kitchen): refuse.
2. Any matter that is no longer wanted or needed, usually in an unmanageable condition, contaminated trash.

Toxic liquid:

1. The unintentional combining of multiple types of waste products (i.e., liquids, solids, animal and vegetable waste).
2. The result of mixing of contaminated liquids to product poisonous waste liquids. Specifically that which accumulates in black liner garbage bags.

Icexit:

1.   The rate at which ice melts from ice-capped lands.
2.   The amount of ice we waste on a daily basis.
3.   The amount of water we put into creating toxic lake.

Let us be clear that when it comes to trash and garbage we are talking about two different things. Trash is actually the byproduct of a billion-, trillion-dollar industry (i.e., packaging, everything that is sold is contained within packaging, with regards to the food industry).

Packaging is mandated by law. It is essential that everything that's sold to a customer be packaged properly; thus, an awfully great amount of energy, effort, and money go into packaging. Packaging usually is made from our earth's natural resources. Like trees, silver, iron, gold and other natural resources which we spend billions of dollars to find, dig up, grow, or harvest in the first place, these raw materials that have value and can be recycled, remolded and easily transformed into other packaging or products. That's what recycling is all about, giving packaging another life, getting two uses out of our most valuable limited resources.

Most packaging is not garbage and should not be placed in bags destined for garbage or landfill applications. Many items of packaging can be washed and returned for effective customer use over and over again, unless damaged.

Garbage, on the other hand, is something destined for landfills and places out of sight, as it is mostly stuff that we don't want to deal with on a daily basis. Even though garbage is unsightly and generally a mess, it's becoming essentially necessary that we deal with garbage versus discarding it into our landfills as we are running out of space to put and place landfills.

Focusing on restaurants and food preparation and packaging, there are many things that go into the black garbage bag that don't belong there.

We at OMT, "One Man's Trash" are out to change the way you think about trash, with a focus on the "aftermeal" waste creation and dissemination, thusly recycling.

Considering all of the above, have we been doing it wrong? Considering that there is more liquids in garbage than solids does it make sense to put them both in the same black liner bag? Because liquids weigh more than paper in the black liner bag, does it still make sense to put them both in the same bag? Considering that the black liner bag was created over 85 years ago with no afterthought, no improvements in the process since 1930, isn't it time we gave more than two shakes of a donkey's tail about black liner bags? About the problem that the single bag collection system for solids, liquid waste collection and all has created?

There are many portals of pollution that exist today, but there is one that's been staring us right in the face on a daily basis, one so simple that if we just only open our eyes and stop and think for a second—that is all that it would take—we would see it. An extra few seconds to solve one of the world's worst most previously unnoticeable problems we have created simply by being lazy. Yes, but we do it. Every single day.

After years of research and observation and just simply looking around at what is happening on our streets and city and businesses with respect to garbage, we noticed that one of the most aggressive of polluters is the restaurant industry. They have an untethered ability to create waste because of the almost very necessary default position that they possess in this country, one of providing our very sustenance, our varied food supply on a daily basis. That we overlook the problem that exists in most restaurants. They use water constantly to cook, clean, prepare our foods. We want them to be sanitary as one mistake in cleanliness could be catastrophic to many people. By law, they have to have bathroom facilities. They have to provide free water to every patron who requests it or not.

Many restaurants who prepare food often use garbage disposal units that grind up leftover food items and flush the remains away, adding to freshwater demands.

Each patron has to be provided with this clean sanitary environment for breakfast, lunch, and dinner. Daily, American restaurants collectively create a great lake of ice for drinking water and other beverage consumption. This is very necessary though, as many of our drinks are prepared for the purpose of including ice. The only problem with this is what we do with it just after we are finished drinking. This is equal to 113 trillion, million gallons of water per day that usually gets thrown away, literally. Very fresh water, in the form of ice, bypasses our sewer system going straight to black liner bags in the form of cups of ice, thusly contributing to the leachate filling our landfills. Yes, the majority of weight in garbage is water; the majority of space used in garbage is from cups.

We are going to focus on that one main problem as we see it here: the aftermeal. What's left after every meal. The leftovers; that piece of plastic fork, knife, spoon; that napkin; those leftover bones; and, most importantly, that undrunk cup of water and ice that you left on the table, probably still having the lid and straw in it. That is called unused, wasted, or, in technical terms, potable water or gray water. Today, everywhere that you can look and see, in every restaurant and street corner, you will find that cup with ice still in it in the garbage can.

Every time that black liner bag gets at least twenty cups in it the bag has to be emptied because it's full now.

We recognize that the mixing of water in the form of ice or soda with paper, animal, and vegetable waste products cause toxic liquids as garbage to accumulate in the bottom of most black liner bags. Because modern waste collection systems have not improved since the creation of the black liner bag, some ninety-plus-years ago. Because modern waste retrieval collection systems do not provide proper liquid receptor mechanisms to deal with liquids. Even though the majority of weight in garbage is water.

Up until now, what was seen to be the greatest way to sanitarily deal with the collection of trash since modern civilization. Until now, what was once the easiest and quickest way to clean up and get rid of the aftermeal was to put it all quickly into the black liner bag and set it out on the curb. There it will stay and sit, soil, and fester, and with the moisture-proof bags, the contents within will start to grow. And depending upon what chemical makeup of the elements that went into the black liner bag will determine what will come out of the black liner bag, only to soil and contaminate everything that it touches.

The contents of the black liner bag once contaminated will remain contaminated for an undeterminable amount of time since its makeup can and will never be determined. It's just called toxic liquid waste now. After liquids mix with all the chemicals and elements within the black liner bag, it is no longer trash. It has now become garbage. Very difficult to recycle, this will stay contaminated for decades now. This is what we are determined to battle; this is why we created the WRC, or the water reclamation canister, to prevent trash from becoming garbage in the first place.

The Makeup of the Aftermeal

In the beginning, it was all taken care of by Mother Nature. Everything has its place. The top predator would make a kill, and they all would wait their turn to eat. The hyena, the jackal, the buzzard all come to eat in their turn, then the insect world would take its time with the remains. Then the fly brings in the maggot, each creature all the way down until the bacterial level has its time at the aftermeal, until it was all gone. Nothing goes to waste in nature. Since everything has always been organic, there has never been a problem with waste control. The earth seemed to bleed then heal itself and then clean up with everyone getting a bit to eat, and so it was. This never-ending story went on for millions of years—until us.

But now today, fast-forward until now. With the creation of such things as the hamburger with fries and a soda. The population explosion. Packaging and food presentation, all food items must come presented with large cup of ice-filled soda or water, a plastic spoon and fork, and napkins. Fast-food restaurants welcomed the invention of the black liner bag and packaging. We have created a world of efficiency in the preservation, delivery, and cleanup of food items. We seem to have fallen into this habit of dealing with the aftermeal, or what's left of our eating habit as fast as possible.

Next time you go to a fast-food place, for example, look at the receipt. Find the customer number or receipt number. Should be some six-digit number indicating how many customers have come through. That generally will tell you how many cups of ice have been sold there. Every meal comes with a burger, fries, and an ice-filled soda, or chicken fries and an ice-filled soda, for everyone. One fact we all have in common is that ice-filled cup of soda. Once you do the math, this is close of an indication as to how many cups of ice normally go straight into the black liner bag once we finished our meal.

In fact, once you open your water tap or faucet all water that goes down the drain, whether you touch, use, or otherwise let it go straight down the drain, it is considered gray water, or potable water. Ice would be considered gray water. Even if never used by anyone, the fact that it has been let out of the faucet tap determines that it is gray water. So each time a patron sits to eat and does not touch the glass of water presented for that meal, that cup of water must be emptied out and a fresh cup of water must be drawn for the new patron. The term *gray water* has various definitions but is typically used to describe water that has flowed through a plumbing system that has not come into contact with feces during its journey. It can come from a sink, bathtub, or washing machine.

We seem to want to through away every little piece of plastic, every little piece of paper, every little plastic straw every time we eat each and every day, three times a day. And we want to be able to get this trash away from us as fast as possible so as to quickly clean up and prepare for the next person. So we all have been taught to use and learned very well the use of the black liner bag. Only problem is what goes around comes around. What goes into the black liner bag does not disappear from existence, it only disappears from sight. That's why they make the color black so you can't see inside of them, what's actually brewing on the inside of the black liner bag. In order to effectively deal with the problems of the bag, we must first look at the contents of the black liner bag.

After some eighty-plus years, we still employ the plastic bag for all types of sanitary garbage collection and removal. But today, the unseen problem that this has created is just now coming to light. It is the fact that the wide and varied types of foods and preprocessed food items that we consume have unforeseen consequences. Let's look at the consequences.

What are the contents of most black liner bags? Bacteria, animal waste, vegetable waste, paper, plastics, ink, bleach, chemicals, dyes, acids, and various types/classes of liquids that don't mix. We understand that the black liner bag is designed for the purpose of sanitarily getting bacteria and waste away from us, but it's just not working as these bags are filling so quickly and spill accrues on the daily. Honestly, black liner bags should be considered handling hazardous material, thusly outlawed. But since that is not likely to happen, we felt that the problem could be dealt with by simply not combining all the above types of waste liquids and solids.

Below, you would find these elements as a basic makeup of contents of elements in the common black liner bag, and values associated with trash. Once we add liquids, water, or soda to the mix, we create poisonous, toxic waste, which is worth nothing.

Pollution opposing viewpoints 2006

On the global level, the fundamental importance of clean water has come into the spotlight. In November 2002, the UN "United Nations" Committee on Economic, Cultural and Social Rights declared access to clean water a human right. Moreover, the United Nations has designated 2003 to be the International Year of Freshwater, with the aim of encouraging sustainable use of freshwater and integrated water resources management.

Implementing the Clean Water Act requires clarifying the sources of pollutants. They are divided into two groups "point sources " and "nonpoint sources." Point sources correspond to discrete, identifiable locations from which pollutants are emitted. They include factories, wastewater treatment plants, landfills, and underground storage tanks. Water pollution that originates at point sources is usually what is associated with headline-grabbing stories such as those about Love Canal.

Nonpoint sources of pollution are diffuse and therefore harder to control. For instance, rain washes oil, grease, and solid pollutants from streets and parking lots into storm drains that carry them into bays and rivers. Likewise, irrigation and rainwater leach fertilizers, herbicides, and insecticides from farms and lawns and into streams and lakes.

The direct discharge of wastes from point sources info lakes rivers, and streams is regulated by a permit program known as the National Pollutant Discharge Elimination System (NPDES). This program, establishes through the Clean Water Act, is administered by the Environmental Protection Agency (EPA) and authorized states. By regulation the wastes discharged, NPDES has helped reduce point-source pollution dramatically, on the other hand, water pollution in the United States is now mainly from nonpoint sources, as reported by the EPA.

Pollution opposing viewpoints 2006

Plastic (1930s). The word *plastic* becomes a part of consumers' everyday language to describe a wide variety of these new materials, a term that continues today. Plastic describes a myriad of items that make up the aftermeal. For example, each and every fast-food restaurant in America has to stock plastic knife, forks, and spoons with complimentary plastic straw too. These items are mandated by law to be available to each customer daily for every meal in order to pass safety inspections.

All these same items of plastic should not be allowed to go into the black liner bag; they should be collected and cleaned effectively and or stored for later pickup by recyclable industries instead of being immediately condemned to the landfill garbage. Plastic should be a recyclable product only and separated from animal and vegetable waste at the time of the aftermeal cleanup. Waiters and waitresses already perform this function for many of us; after every meal, most patrons simply get up and leave, leaving the cleanup to the service personnel. It's why we are encouraged to tip our service personnel. This knowledge of types of recyclable products should be encouraged in our schools and academia for the sake of our environment. Knowledge of this type should equate to management-level job security. We intend to show the value of this type of personnel to a business establishment.

Soft Drinks and the Ice Sector

The soft drinks and ice sector has an estimated global revenue of $676 billion and consumes an estimated thirteen metric tons of plastic packaging, almost 98 percent of which is used in beverage containers containing ice. For every ton of plastic used in the sector, an estimated 7.3 metric tons of alternative materials would be required, including the following:

- 0.1 metric tons of tin plate, steel or iron
- 0.3 metric tons of aluminum
- 6.5 metric tons of glass
- 0.3 metric tons of paper and paperboard

This substitution reduces the sector's average cost per metric ton of material from $1,323 for plastics to $951 for alternatives, but increases the quantity of materials required by 7.3 times and the environmental cost by 5.2 times. This highlights the efficiency of plastics for use in bottling applications compared to glass, the leading market alternative. And all these drinks require ice to condition them prior to our consumption. This is the value of the so-called trash as a raw product, 95 percent of which is recyclable if it can be kept in a recyclable state. Liquid waste products (i.e., poisonous toxins) are created within the black liner bag by mixing solid waste and liquid waste together, which creates garbage.

The Ice Cube Factor

It is not known for certain who invented the ice cube. Dr. John Gorrie built a refrigerator in 1844 to aid his yellow fever patients. Some historians believe that this refrigerator contained some form of ice cube tray because he gave his patients iced drinks.

An ice cube melts faster in water than it does in air, given equal circumstances. Heat energy is needed in order for an ice cube to melt. Heat energy travels faster through water than it does through air.

So after you drink off the liquid, the cube can live up to forty-plus minutes in a cup.

a. An ice cube can weigh up to five-plus grams.
b. A cup of ice cubes can weigh up to more than a pound.
c. Ten cups of ice cubes can weigh up to ten-plus pounds.
d. An average thirty-two–pound black liner bag can contain up to thirty-plus cups of ice cubes and extra forty-plus pounds in each black liner bag.
e. Water makes up 80 percent of *weight* in each black liner bag.
f. Cups take up 60 percent of space in each black liner bag.

The Leaky Faucet ("Icexit")

Ever stop to think about the leaky faucet? We all know that our present-day plumbing system needs upgrading and monitoring. See, every one of us who uses the commercial sewer system, the city water-distribution plumbing system is connected to the plumbing system that we all use, so for example, if someone went on vacation and has a faulty water tap with a leak or drippy faucet, a swimming pool of water could drain through that leak if left unattended. Almost any home connected to the city plumbing system could waste tons of water via a leak. So it is clear as to how much water could be saved by fixing leaks.

Now imagine that an ice cube is a leak, only ten times larger. Imagine a system that collects ice cubes and recirculates them into use. This is a source of "fresh gray water," which has previously been thrown away, overlooked, considered garbage.

In an average day, American restaurants collectively create a great lake of ice for drinking water and other beverage consumption and other cooling uses. This is equal to 113 trillion, million gallons of water per day that bypasses our sewer system, going straight to black liner bags, thusly our landfills, where it becomes a part of toxic waste water, where the technical term *leachate* is used to describe the great lake of toxic poison that we just created. Toxic waste does not grow naturally; we create it. It's a man- or woman-made entity. We do this on the daily.

One could almost think of ice as a natural resource like trees, for example we grow and harvest trees, use them once and attempt to recycle them. We do the same with most other natural resources. Well we can almost look at ice in same manner, we make it, harvest it, and use it once and throw it away, right into the garbage can with lid and straw and ice still in the cup. This is first part of the problem.

As you will come to know, our landfills are trying to accommodate this great lake of toxic poison. Thinking that we can build these structures leakproof, that we have to contain this lake of toxic leachate in the first place is the second problem. We should avoid creating this toxic lake in the first place. They, landfills, are the perfect storm waiting to happen; just as soon as a good tornado or hurricane happens, the leachate flows, just as soon as water is added. These poisons flow in great masses, toward our lakes and streams, thusly getting into our oceans.

This is a great toil on our earth as it speeds up the effect of global warming. This is equal to the average amount of ice that melts from our polar-capped territories on a daily basis. The polar ice caps melt, and the loss of natural resources of unrecycled ice equal out. And both are very preventable. Our waste collection system is over eighty years old, hasn't changed since the invention of plastic.

The time has come to upgrade the waste-collection system, to modernize the waste-collection system. It begins at the hands of the user: you. It begins with education. It begins with recognizing the value of what we throw away.

The first thing we need to look at is our very own eating habits. One thing we all have in common in whatever we eat is the enormous mess that we create. It's called the aftermeal, the stuff that's left over after we finish a great meal, any meal. What's left is the stuff of poison. Toxic poisoning. Let's look at the makeup of the ingredients that go into the bag, which contributes to the problem.

Chemical/Ingredient Makeup of Common Foods

Common butter: Butter fats are a mixture of triglycerides of different fatty acids. Oleic, myristic, palmitic, and stearic acids make up about 80 percent of these fatty acids. Lauric, butyric, caproic, capric, linolenic, and linoleic acids make up the remainder of the fatty acids in butter fat. The short-chain butyric acid contributes most prominently to the flavor of uncooked butter. The milk solids in butter include proteins and molecules such as carotenoids, which cause the yellow coloration of butter, and methyl ketones and lactones, which contribute to the flavor profile of dishes made with cooked butter.

Artificial sweeteners: Such as acesulfame potassium, sucralose, and saccharin. Aspartame.

Artificial flavors: Strawberry artificial flavor can contain nearly fifty chemical ingredients, also an artificial flavoring called diacetyl.

MSG: Is an excitotoxin, which means it overexcites your cells to the point of damage or death, causing brain dysfunction and damage to varying degrees, and potentially even triggering or worsening learning disabilities, Alzheimer's disease, Parkinson's disease, Lou Gehrig's disease, and more. Free glutamic acid (MSG is approximately 78 percent–free glutamic acid).

Artificial colors: Every year, food manufacturers pour fifteen million pounds of artificial food dyes into US foods—and that amount only factors in eight different varieties. As of July 2010, most foods in the European Union that contain artificial food dyes were labeled with warning labels stating the food "may have an adverse effect on activity and attention in children." The British government also asked that food manufacturers remove most artificial colors from foods back in 2009 due to health concerns. Nine of the food dyes currently approved for use in the United States are linked to health issues ranging from cancer and hyperactivity to allergy-like reactions.

High-fructose corn syrup (HFCS): It's often claimed that HFCS is no worse for you than sugar, but this is not the case. Because high-fructose corn syrup contains free-form monosaccharides of fructose and glucose, it cannot be considered biologically equivalent to sucrose (sugar).

Preservatives: Preservatives lengthen the shelf life of foods, increasing manufacturers' profits—at your expense, since most are linked to health problems such as cancer, allergic reactions, and more. Butylated hydroxyanisole (BHA) and butylated hydrozyttoluene (BHT) are preservatives that affect the neurological system of your brain, alter behavior, and have the potential to cause cancer. Tertiary butylhydroquinone (TBHQ) is a chemical preservative so deadly that just five grams of it can kill you.

The preservative sodium benzoate—found in many soft drinks, fruit juices, and salad dressings—has been found to cause children to become measurably more hyperactive and distractible. Sodium nitrite, a commonly used preservative in hot dogs, deli meats, and bacon, has been linked to higher rates of colorectal, stomach, and pancreatic cancers. And the list goes on and on.

US-Processed Foods May Be Even Worse than Those in Other Countries

Many of the food additives that are perfectly legal to use in US foods are banned in other countries. The banned ingredients include various food dyes, the fat substitute olestra, brominated vegetable oil, potassium bromate (a.k.a. brominanted flour), azodicarbonamide, BHA, BHT, rBGH, rBST, and arsenic.

As you can see, American food packaging and food preparation can contain many of the above-mentioned ingredients, which wind up in our black liner bags, which when mixed with water in the form of ice or other varied types of liquids can result in varied mixtures and types of liquids otherwise described as toxins, very poisonous toxins, most of which may never be duplicated so as to be allowed to be tested for the various cancers or diseases that they may cause or create. The poisonous toxins that are created are even having major consequences in nature as they leak out into puddles created once garbage bags are not picked up and these poisonous toxins are allowed to accumulate in small puddles and small lakes and water actuaries, and are killing insect and water aquatic life that depend on these waters.

These black liner bags full of poisonous toxins in our restaurants are creating on a daily basis, every day once we mix our solid trash with our liquid waste, this results in our poisonous-toxins lake creation that we discussed earlier. Once the ice melts and mixes with other stuff, it's too late. Toxins have been created.

We at OMT are on a mission to bring light to this problem that affects our world. Here in California the environmental effect of plastic shopping bag has been analyzed and already outlawed. Case studies would suggest that black liner bags should be next or first on the list to be outlawed, or they should be porous in type so as not to collect poisonous toxins, thereby keeping trash as trash that can one day be recycled. We at OMT are designing and focusing on building waste management systems to facilitate the recycling industry in mind and development.

Here are four things about plastics recycling you may not know:

1. *Recyclers want your caps and lids.* Don't throw your soft drink bottle caps in the trash can, or your butter tub lids either. They're not trash! Bottle caps and container lids are made with valuable plastics, and recyclers want them too. Simply put caps and lids back on bottles and containers and toss them in the recycling bin together. Recyclers typically shred them all into flakes and then submerge the flakes in water. Bottle flakes sink and the other flakes float, making it easy to separate the plastics for recycling. Optical scanners and other technologies can help too.

2. *Used packaging isn't only recycled into new packaging.* While used plastic packaging sometimes is recycled to make new packaging, this isn't always the case. Used plastic milk jugs, for example, often are recycled into playground equipment, patio furniture, cooking tools, and more. And plastic yogurt containers can become reusable food storage containers, floor rugs, tableware, and other cool products.

3.   *Bottles can become clothing.* Many clothing designers today use fabrics made from recycled plastic bottles to make a variety of clothing, from fancy dresses to comfortable T-shirts to rugged fleece jackets to board shorts. The bottles are cleaned, shredded, heated, and then stretched into fine threads that are woven into soft, durable fabrics. These recycled fabrics can be manufactured with different weights and textures to provide a range of design options.

4.   *Plastic bags and wraps can be recycled at thousands of locations.* It's easier than ever to recycle dry-cleaning bags, food wraps, food storage bags, grocery store bags, product wraps, and more. Clean and dry bags and wraps are collected for recycling at more than eighteen thousand grocery and retail stores nationwide, but usually not curbside. Manufacturers turn these plastics into new bags and other products—in fact, your used plastic bag could become part of your new backyard deck.

The Circular Economy (Source: Trucost)

Moving to a more circular economy can reduce the environmental costs of plastics. The circular economy is an alternative to the traditional linear make-use-dispose economic model, which prioritizes the extension of product life cycles, extracting maximum value from resources in use, and then recovering materials at the end of their service life. An important principle of the circular economy is increasing the capture and recovery of materials in waste streams so that they can be recycled and reused in new products. Increasing the recycling of postconsumer plastics (to 55 percent) and minimizing landfilling (to a maximum of 10 percent) could deliver significant environmental benefits.

If these targets were implemented across Europe and North America, the environmental cost of plastics could be reduced by over $7.9 billion in net terms, accounting for the increased environmental impacts associated with waste collection and management, and in addition to the direct economic gains associated with the recovered value of recycled plastics and recovered energy. Recycling delivers a social and environmental return on investment on top of the economic value of recovered materials, with the environmental benefits of increasing recycling in this scenario outweighing the costs of pollution emissions and external waste management costs by at least 3.9 times.

Effect on Our Oceans (Source: Trucost)

Capturing plastic waste before it reaches the ocean could cut ocean costs by over $2.1 billion.

Improving waste collection and management is key to reducing the quantity of plastics entering the ocean each year along with the resulting environmental costs. Asia, with its large and growing consumer goods market and comparably low municipal waste-collection rates, is estimated to contribute over 70 percent of the total quantity of plastic reaching the ocean from the consumer goods sector each year. Trucost estimates that by increasing the municipal waste collection rate in Asia to a GDP weighted average of 80 percent, the annual global plastic input to the oceans could be cut by over 45 percent (1.1 metric tons) and save $2.1 billion in environmental costs.

Looking ahead, we can see similar investments in waste management infrastructure will be critical in Africa, where incomes are rising and waste management systems remain poor. As incomes rise, waste-generation rates (including plastic waste) are expected to increase with significant implications for the world's oceans. However, it is important to note that without commensurate improvements in material and energy recovery, the ocean cost benefits of better waste collection could be offset by increased environmental disamenity and public costs of waste management.

So as one can see, there is a vast untapped financial market in waste management systems that capture plastic and paper trash prior to it reaching our rivers, streams, and oceans. This is where OMT has positioned itself within the industry.

The global oceans are critical to sustaining the earth's natural life support systems. They contribute to the livelihoods, culture, and well-being of communities around the world and play a vital role in the global economy, providing food and a source of income for millions of people. Yet with a fast-growing world population, the production of waste continues to increase faster than the efforts mitigate its impact on the oceans. The production of toxins from ice water is just coming into vision and reality. Its effect should not and cannot be underestimated, for it poisons the very land-born and water-born life so very necessary for all our very being, as all life depends on clean water. The very first step toward elimination of toxins is to stop mixing liquid and solid waste products.

More mismanaged waste means more marine litter, and it has been estimated that 80 percent of marine debris originates from land-based sources (Jambeck et al. 2015) with the remaining 20 percent originating from ocean-based sources (Allsopp et al., n.d.). Land-based sources include storm-water discharges, combined sewer overflows, littering, industrial activities, and solid-waste disposal and landfills. Debris from such sources are often washed, blown, or discharged into waterways from rainfall, snowmelt, and wind (Sheavly and Register 2007). In the case of both land- and ocean-based sources, poor waste handling practices, both legal and illegal, contribute to marine debris (ibid).

Plastic is the most common form of marine debris. Estimates have put the average proportion of plastic marine debris between 60 to 80 percent of all marine debris (Moore 2008). In some places, the proportion can be as high as 90–95 percent of all marine debris (ibid). Plastic is frequently used in single-use packaging application, which are rapidly disposed and at risk of entering the marine environment if improperly managed (Jambeck et al. 2015).

Plastics in the marine environment can also persist longer than some other materials due to their durability and resistance to natural biodegradation processes. Plastics can potentially persist for years to decades, or even longer in the ocean (Law et al. 2010). However, the true life span of plastics has been difficult estimate. In many instances, plastics will not fully degrade and instead break down into smaller and smaller pieces, eventually becoming microplastics, or plastics that measure less than 5 mm. (Source: Trucost)

Plastics and Sustainability

Marine debris can cause a variety of problems, posing environmental, economic, and health risks. Environmental risks include entanglement of marine animals, ingestion by marine animals, and the spread of invasive species. Ingested debris can block the digestive tract or fill the stomach of wildlife, resulting in malnutrition, starvation, reduced reproductive capacity, general reduction in quality of life, or death (Gregory 2016). Floating debris can travel great distances, potentially carrying invasive species with it, introducing them to new ecosystems where they have the potential to compete with native species (Sheavly and Register 2007). Marine debris on beaches reduces tourism and recreational use of these areas, thus decreasing their economic value (ibid).

In addition, the cleanup of marine debris is costly to governments and businesses, and presents an economic opportunity cost where volunteers engage in cleanup activities, and larger debris pieces can damage vessels resulting in costly repairs and loss of time (ibid). Fish and invertebrates can ingest microplastics, potentially leading to the bioaccumulation of plastic additives and hazardous organic chemicals absorbed from the environment, within the food chain presenting potential risks for human consumption health (Rochman et al. 2013).

More recent research, however, suggests that the bioaccumulation of hazardous organic chemicals due to plastic ingested by marine life is small compared to bioaccumulation in prey species in most habitats. This suggests that microplastic ingestion may not increase exposure to hazardous organic chemicals in the marine environment (Koelmans et al. 2016).

Nevertheless, quantifying the amount of marine debris entering the ocean is important for understanding its full economic and environmental cost and impacts. Interest and research efforts into the issue of ocean plastic have increased significantly in recent years. In 2015, a seminal paper by Jambeck et al. (2015) was published in the journal *Science* that described a methodology for quantifying the input of plastic into the oceans from land-based sources.

This model considered the quantities of unmanaged waste generated by coastal populations (within 50 km of the coast) and developed a model describing the conversion rate for land-based litter into marine debris. This paper culminated in the best estimate to date of the annual inflow of plastic waste into the ocean at between 4.8 and 12.7 mt globally. Building on this research, and other recent developments in marine debris research. Reducing Food Waste in Packaged Meat Products. This one could only conclude that many of the plastic bags contained liquids that did not escape the bag, suggesting that the above numbers qualify as liquid waste included in or part of our man-made toxic lake created from mixing liquids with solid waste in our very own black liner bags.

The UN Food and Agriculture Organization Food Waste

The UN Food and Agriculture Organization (FAO 2011) estimates that around one-third of all food produced is lost or wasted globally. Food loss can occur throughout the supply chain from farm- and processing-stage losses through wasted food in retail outlets and households. While food loss in developing countries and industrialized countries are equally likely to occur, they tend to occur at different stages of the supply chain (FAO 2011). In developing countries, more than 40 percent of food loss occurs at the postharvest and processing levels, whereas in industrialized countries about 40 percent of food loss happens at the retail or consumer level (ibid). In the United States, for example, 31 percent of the available food supply at the retail and consumer level is wasted (Buzby, Wells, and Hyman 2014).

Besides the lost economic value of wasted food, the natural resources and environmental impacts involved in producing the wasted food are also lost. The scale of these resources and impacts can be staggering. In the United States, food production accounts for 80 percent of all freshwater use (USDA 2015a), 51 percent of land use (USDA, 2015b), and 15 percent of the country's energy budget (USDA 2012). Food waste, therefore, accounts for 25 percent of all US freshwater use and 4 percent of total US oil consumption (NRDC 2013). In addition to the environmental cost of lost resources, most food waste end up in landfills, where it releases methane gas as it decomposes.

The carbon footprint of food waste is estimated at 3.3 billion metric tons of CO_2e, with cereals and meat accounting for 34 percent and 21 percent of that footprint respectively (FAO 2013). Approximately 60 percent of household food waste arises from products not used due to being perishable or having a short shelf life (WRAP 2016). One of the most effective ways to extend shelf life and reduce food waste is through packaging. Research has shown that how long food stays fresh is a priority for consumers. Packaging innovations such as modified atmosphere packaging (MAP) and vacuum skin packaging (VSP) have been shown to extend freshness (Denkstatt 2015). Continued innovation and adoption of new packaging technology could further shelf life extension and reduce household food waste, thereby curbing greenhouse gas emissions and natural resources lost to food waste.

In this case study, Trucost examines the potential environmental cost savings associated with packaging to reduce the waste of beef, one of the most environmentally costly food products. This analysis builds upon a study by Denkstatt (2015), which quantified the reduction in food waste achieved through different types of packaging for sirloin steak. The case study considers two options for packaging sirloin steak:

- Conventional packaging, including an expanded polystyrene tray sealed with plastic film with a modified atmosphere.
- Improved composite (polystyrene, ethylene vinyl acetate, and polyethylene) skin packaging that can extend the shelf life of the steak by six to sixteen days and reduce food

waste. This packaging also allows the steak to be cut and aged in the package, reducing the need for separate aging packing (Denkstatt 2015). The environmental impact associated with the production and disposal of the packaging material and the production and treatment of waste beef was estimated to assess the net change in impacts associated with the shift in packaging-type change in environmental costs through the use of improved plastic packaging. The net reduction in environmental costs is estimated at $606 per metric ton of steak, primarily due to avoided environmental costs associated with the production of beef that is ultimately wasted.

For consistency with other components of this study, this analysis included only environmental costs associated with greenhouse gas emissions, water consumption and the emission of air, land and water pollution. It does not include the costs of land occupation, which can be extensive in beef cattle production. A recent study for the FAO undertaken by Trucost (FAO 2015) found that the conversion of natural land to pasture for beef production could account for 75 percent of the environmental cost of production.

What Types of Landfills Are There?

Although our landfills are usually constructed with the greatest of design and material, spills and leaks happen usually in the ungodliest of places and times. Never can they be accounted for, and the spill is always an accident. They boast of being able to collect the leachate and store it sufficiently.

The problem is when the government gets involved it has to do things on a grand scale. Diverting crap from the landfills is tedious work; it usually requires a little more than just two shakes of a donkey's tail. Leachate from landfills contain an unlimited amount of minerals and poisons that we never dreamed of combining before. It results in that each time it rains which introduces more liquid water to a landfill, resulting in more leachate, which is the culmination of all the elements of a landfill, which includes metals, bacteria, organic, inorganic, explosive, and nonexplosive types of elements.

The EPA department of consumer affairs only has seventy-two known chemical components that they are trying to track and control and/or eliminate use of. What happens when some of those chemicals mix? What makes up leachate in a landfill should never be allowed to exist, nor can we ever hope to continually deal with trying to develop new methods of deactivating this poison.

Landfills are regulated under RCRA Subtitle D (solid waste) and Subtitle C (hazardous waste) or under the Toxic Substances Control Act (TSCA). Subtitle D focuses on state and local governments as the primary planning, regulating, and implementing entities for the management of nonhazardous solid waste, such as household garbage and nonhazardous industrial solid waste.

Subtitle D landfills include the following:

- Municipal Solid Waste Landfills (MSWLFs)—Specifically designed to receive household waste, as well as other types of nonhazardous wastes.
- Bioreactor Landfills—A type of MSWLF that operates to rapidly transform and degrade organic waste.
- Industrial Waste Landfill—Designed to collect commercial and institutional (i.e. industrial waste), which is often a significant portion of solid waste, even in small cities and suburbs.
- Construction and Demolition (C&D) Debris Landfill—A type of industrial waste landfill designed exclusively for construction and demolition materials, which consists of the debris generated during the construction, renovation and demolition of buildings, roads and bridges. C&D materials often contain bulky, heavy materials, such as concrete, wood, metals, glass, and salvaged building components.

- Coal Combustion Residual (CCR) landfills—An industrial waste landfill used to manage and dispose of coal combustion residuals (CCRs or coal ash). EPA established requirements for the disposal of CCR in landfills and published them in the Federal Register April 17, 2015.

Subtitle C establishes a federal program to manage hazardous wastes from cradle to grave. The objective of the Subtitle C program is to ensure that hazardous waste is handled in a manner that protects human health and the environment. To this end, there are Subtitle C regulations for the generation, transportation and treatment, storage or disposal of hazardous wastes.

Subtitle C landfills including the following:

- Hazardous Waste Landfills—Facilities used specifically for the disposal of hazardous waste. These landfills are not used for the disposal of solid waste.

CHAPTER 2

The Answer, Composting

Options Other Than Landfills

From UC ANR Master Gardener Program:

From Cal Recycle (formerly CIWMB):

In 2010, California's estimated 38.3million residents disposed about 31.1 million tons of solid waste for an estimated statewide per capita disposal rate of 4.5 pounds/person/day. Forty percent of this waste is classified as "Other organic," which means it's compostable.

What can we do as individuals? Everything. It's all up to us; it's our habits that got us into this mess, it will be our habits that get us out. Firstly, you can start by separating your waste items. Secondly, you can start a composting bin in your yard or house. Very easy to do; get to know your friendly earthworm and the value they possess. But firstly, we need to stop poisoning the earth each and every day so that we may provide a better habitat that all of God's creatures can continue to live and thrive in earth's soil.

Our mission presently is to bring light to today's plight of our bad habit of poisoning ourselves. By increasing focus on composting and gaining more knowledge about alternatives to landfills, we should educate ourselves on ways of the world. Falling back on my master gardener experience, below are some tips to conserving the earth's resources through conservation and proper living.

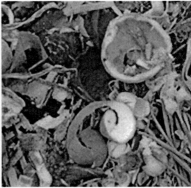

Turning waste into a resource.

• Rapidly depleting landfill capacity, low potential for California landfill expansion, more and more waste!

Goal: Divert waste from landfills and recycle it.

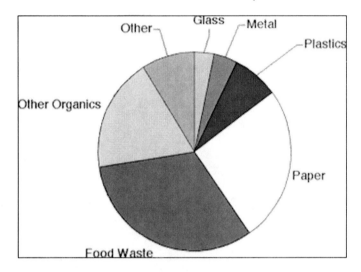

Environmental benefits:

• Waste reduction
• Keeps soil fertile
• Air quality
• Resource conservation (water)

Gardening benefits:

• Saves money
• Enriches soil
• Contributes to a healthy lifestyle

Compost Processes and Critters in the Compost Pile

A compost pile is an ecosystem of various creatures and elements. The function is one of decomposition of organic matter into stable humus.

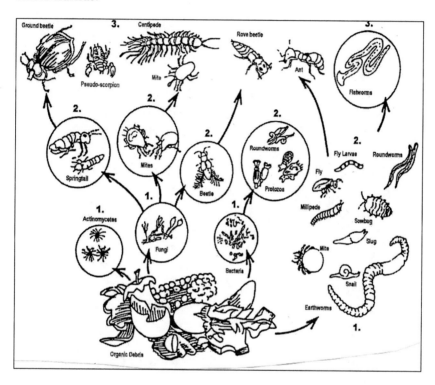

The compost process depends on the following:

- Organic matter composition
- Carbon (browns)
- Nitrogen (greens)
- Microorganisms
- Macroorganisms
- Water
- Oxygen
- Temperature

Organic Matter: Carbon, or "Browns"

Carbon-rich sources are called "browns." Usually dry, has low moisture content, lightweight. Examples: dry leaves, straw, sawdust, wood chips, corn stalks.

Organic Matter: Nitrogen, or "Greens"

N is needed to get the decomposition process started and keep the pile "cookin'." Examples: vegetable and fruit scraps, grass clippings, coffee grounds, manures, and alfalfa hay
Carbon-Nitrogen Ratio
Optimal C:N ratio is 30:1 at an elemental level.
Carbon supplies energy for bacteria, and nitrogen supplies nutrients (proteins).

Balance material ratios to get 30:1 ratio:

1/5 oak leaves 26:1	1/5 poultry manure 10:1
1/5 pine needles 85:1	1/5/grass clippings 20:1
1/5 food scraps 15:1	C:N ratio = ~31:1

Approximately equal volumes of greens and browns provide a good C:N ratio.

C:N Ratio Explained

The compost pile provides "the energy for the bacteria to accumulate nutrients needed to grow and reproduce." If there is more C than needed: inefficient. They have the energy but hardly any proteins to eat. If there is more N than needed, they don't have the energy to eat it, and it volatilizes.

The Decomposers: Microorganisms

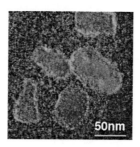

Bacteria begin breakdown process—aerobic bacteria feed on plant sugars and respire to "heat up" pile.

In the right conditions, population growth is amazing; bacteria can double every hour!

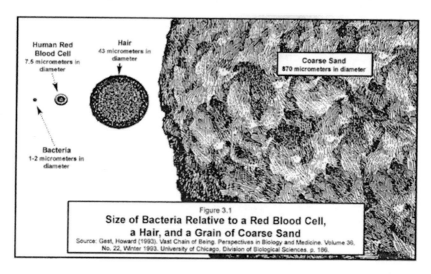

Figure 3.1
Size of Bacteria Relative to a Red Blood Cell, a Hair, and a Grain of Coarse Sand
Source: Gest, Howard (1993). Vast Chain of Being. Perspectives in Biology and Medicine. Volume 36, No. 22, Winter 1993. University of Chicago. Division of Biological Sciences. p. 186.

More microorganisms:

- Fungi: Active in end stages of composting; live on dead or dying material.
- Actinomycetes: Halfway between bacteria and fungi; gray-white cobweb type material in compost pile, also active in later stages of composting.

Microorganisms

As temperatures decline, population diversity increases:

Nematodes: sightless, brainless roundworms, <1 mm long. Prey on bacteria, protozoa, fungal spores

Fermentation or mold mites

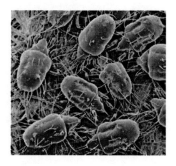

Springtails, tiny white insects

Macroorganisms

Wolf spiders: build no webs, run free hunting their prey.

Centipedes: flattened body, long legs, fast moving.

Millipedes: wormlike body with hard plated, up to six inches long. Slow-moving vegetarians that help in breaking down OM.

Sow bugs and pill bugs (isopods): small, fat-bodied decomposers with gills. Pill bugs roll ingo a ball, sow bugs don't. Feed on rotting woody materials.

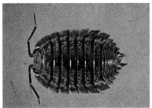 

Beetles: rove beetle, ground beetle, and feather-winged beetle

Earthworms: native redworms

Enchytraeids (ehn kee tray'id): white or pot worms, one-fourth to an inch long, white and segmented.

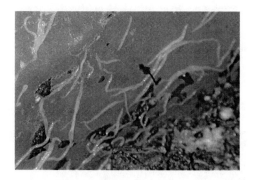

Flies: feed on any organic matter. Bury kitchen scraps well, and keep fatty foods out of the pile to control.

Oxygen

Aerobic composting is preferable.

Anaerobic decomposition or fermentation may produce compounds toxic to plants. Produces ammonia and methane gas—smelly.

Passive aeration: air is warmed by the compost process, rises through the pile, and pulls in fresh air from sides.

Active aeration: turn and mix the compost, or build the pile effectively so surface air diffuses in the pile.

How Long Does It Take?

It depends on the following: density of material, particle size (amount of exposed area), carbon and nitrogen content, moisture content, aeration, volume.

Insulating Material around the Pile

What kind of bin should I use?

What goes in the pile?

Grass clippings, yard waste, leaves, pine needles, vegetable trimmings, food scraps, wood chips shredded to size, newsprint, sawdust.

What does *not* go into the pile?

Disease-infected plants, plants with severe insect attack, ivy, morning glory, and succulents. Pernicious weeds (i.e., bermuda grass, oxalis, cheeseweed). Cat and dog manure. Meat and fish scraps. Wood ash (add after composting is finished).

Vermiculture

Composting with worms.
Ideal for small spaces.
Good for small amounts of green waste food scraps.
Requires less physical activity, little effort.
Produces excellent soil amendment.

What Is Vermiculture?

Red worms transform decaying organic matter into worm castings
Also known as vermicomposting or worm composting
Casting contains available plant nutrients

Not "hot" composting

But a University of Wisconsin research has shown that pathogens and weed seeds can be killed by worms, usually done in containers, indoors, or outdoors.

Composting Worms

Two main species:

Most common *Eisenia fetida*, the most common composting worm because it processes large amounts of organic matter. In ideal conditions, it eats its body weight daily. It reproduces rapidly and is tolerant of variations in growing conditions.

Next: *Lumbricus rubellus.*
A.k.a. red wrigglers and red worms.

Red worms are not soil-dwelling worms; they require large amounts of organic material.

Natives of litter layers of forests, manure piles, and backyard compost heaps.

Night crawlers are not suitable for worm composting; they dig burrows and require lots of soil.

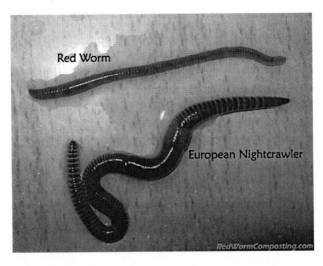

Worm Anatomy

They have no eyes, but are sensitive to light. No ears, but are sensitive to vibrations. They have five hearts, no teeth; they have a gizzard, which contains small grains of sand and mineral particles. They use muscular contractions to grind food. They breathe through their skins and have no lungs; their skin must stay moist to allow it to respire, or they will die.

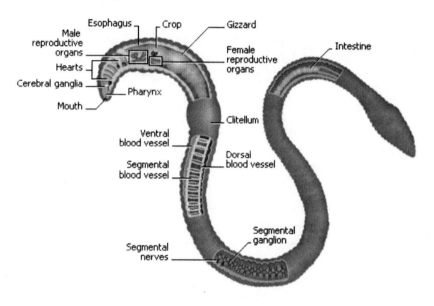

Worm Anatomy and Reproduction

Hermaphrodites, equipped with both male and female organs. When conditions are favorable, a mature red worm (two months old) mates and produces two to three cocoons per week. Two to five baby worms hatch from each cocoon.

Cocoons are lemon shaped, and are the size of a match head.

Worm reproduction facts: they are very prolific, but they understand population control. If worms are removed for starting another worm bin, population quickly returns to its former level.

They tolerate a wide temperature range, preferably temperatures between 55–77 F. They need good air circulation and like moist—but not wet—environments.

They eat between half to a hundred of their full weight in organic material per day. So on an average, a pound of red worms will process about half a pound of food scraps per day.

What do worms eat? Vegetable and fruit scraps, pasta, and bread. Leftover aftermeal stuff like cereal, eggshells (crushed up). They love coffee grounds and filter paper, tea leaves, tea bags, paper towels, napkins, newspapers, manure from cows and horses; rabbit dung and guinea pig droppings are a treat.

What not to put into the worm bin are seeds not broken down, woody yard waste, citrus peels, animal byproducts like cheese, oils, bones, meat. And especially no herbicide-treated plants.

End from UC ANR Master Gardener Program

Amazing Facts about the Earthworm

Imagine a worker who can aerate your soil while fertilizing, soil conditioning, liming, and creating humus. This same creature can mineralize soil and repopulate beneficial biology while also improving structure. If your soil contains good numbers of these workers, then it is a good indication that you have a happy and productive soil food web. It has been suggested that the presence of this remarkable life form can be seen as a marker of the success and sustainability of any given society. I refer here to the humble earthworm.

The earthworm offers exactly that kind of edge. The presence of these remarkable life forms in your soil heralds a disease suppressive soil with more carbon-building potential and less requirement for chemical intervention. The food produced on these soils will be more nutrient dense and the cost of production significantly less.

The earthworm is such a familiar creature that it is rarely given a second thought, yet its contribution to soil fertility is enormous. They tunnel through the ground, eating their way through the soil. They also drag leaves and other plant debris down into the soil, which allows air to enter it and water to drain through. Their activities over millions of years have been vital in creating rich, fertile soils from dense, infertile clays.

Many animals get their food from the soil, but the earthworm eats the soil itself. It crunches it up in its muscular stomach, digests what it can (the organic material that is mixed with the mineral fragments), and ejects the rest.

Earthworms cast from one square meter of meadow were weighed over the course of one year. It emerged that the worms brought about 8 kg of soil to the surface annually.

Panning for Gold:

A short time ago, when we lived on the farm in Modesto, I used to sell worms. Among other things such as guinea pigs, rabbits, plants and fertilizers. I would grow worms "wrigglers and night crawlers" in bins and in the ground. One day me and a good friend of mine went panning for gold in the Nevada area, one of the local rivers there known for having gold runs in the past. As we cleared out an area in the riverbed to get below the rocky river bottom, to the dirt to start the panning process you know. Each time I would dig my panning bowl to gather bottom sand and soil to filter for gold nuggets I kept coming up with these worms in my pan. These worms were living in the bottom soil of a riverbed. Yes getting plenty of fresh oxygen, water and nutrients from below the worms were thriving there in the riverbed. Then and there I came up with a new product. Liquid worm castings. I went home got a 500 gallon plastic water container, bought some cotton bags with string ties, filled these bags with rabbit dung and 4 – 500 live redworms in the bags and submerged this into 100 gallons of water with an aeration bar in the water to keep oxygen flowing throughout. The result was the best worm fertilizer ever made. The process worked great, we sold some to local growers and neighbors too. This is what we used to put on our plants grown on the farm to keep them healthy and pest free. You see so the earthworm is very versatile creature, they can live in a small environment so long as the food, oxygen and moisture holds out.

As the earthworm spends most of its life underground, ploughing through the soil and creating complex burrow networks (that may extend two meters or more beneath the surface), their bodies are basically like a tube of muscle arranged in two layers. One set of fibers run lengthways, and another run widthways, like a corset around its body. Tightening the "corset" forces the worm's head forward. A wave of contractions then passes back down the body, squeezing more of the worm forward until the long muscles take over to pull up the tail.

Worm Castings

Worm castings (a.k.a. worm manure, vermicomposting, or worm excreta) are rich in plant nutrients, trace minerals, and growth enhancers, and incorporating castings into the soil significantly increases microbial life in the root zone. Worm castings are extremely beneficial in that they stimulate plant growth more than any other natural product, enhance the ability of your soil to retain water, and also inhibit root diseases such as root rot. The humus in worm castings removes toxins and harmful fungi and bacteria from the soil. Worm castings, therefore, have the ability to fight off plant diseases.

One of the best features of worm castings is you can use as much as you want without the fear of burning tender young plants, as other fertilizers are known to do. Unlike other animal manure and artificial fertilizers, it is absorbed very easily and almost instantaneously by plants. The amazing thing is that while the nutrients are easily available, they are at the same time naturally endowed with a slow-release feature, causing the nutrient benefits to last up to two months! This benefit is put in place during the digestion process of the earthworm.

As the organic matter passes through the alimentary canal of the worm, a thin layer of oil coats the material, later eroding over a period of two months. The best of both worlds, immediate and long-lasting benefits! Ordinary composts do not have this benefit; they are placed in the garden to enrich the soil and plants, and the available nutrients are quickly leached into the soil as soon as rainfall occurs or irrigation systems are turned on. Vermicompost provides a time-released benefit, slowly nurturing the plants over a greater length of time!

Another natural benefit of worm castings is the ability to fix heavy metals in organic waste, preventing plants from absorbing more of these chemical compounds than they need. The compounds can then be released later when the plants need them. A natural protection for plants set in place by the Creator!

You need only use a small amount in or around your house plants, vegetables, and flowers, as the humic acid in worm castings are able to stimulate plant growth, even in low concentrations. Humic acid also stimulates the development of micro flora populations in the soil. The miracles of the earthworm are easily seen in the beautiful growth and yields of your plants. With their extremely dark and rich texture, tests on worm castings have shown the nitrogen content to be five times greater than ordinary topsoil, the phosphate seven times greater, potash eleven times, and magnesium three times. Castings will not burn even when applied directly to the most delicate plants. Definitely the finest soil conditioner available. Great for use in your entire garden! Completely odor-free and 100 percent organic! Use for indoor plants and container gardening as well. Mainly on the home front.

All these benefits and more.

Setting Up a Worm Bin

Drill holes in bottom, around sides. Then fill bin with four to six inches of well-moistened bedding; add red worms. You will want to spread worms over the surface of the bedding, the exposed worms will migrate down into the bedding. Once worms are inside the bedding, add food. Bury food product four to six inches inside the bedding, and rotate food placement in the bin until you understand their food-consumption rate. Worms will adjust to their new environment, so add food in small amounts at first.

Critters in the Bin

Critters can include springtails, spiders, centipedes, millipedes, sow bugs and pill bugs, echtraeids, mites, fruit flies, ants, slugs, snails, and beetles.

Harvesting Castings

As worm castings increase, the worms' environment quality declines; when much of the bedding in the box becomes castings, the worm population will suffer.

Castings should be harvested before the bedding is completely converted to castings.

By focusing on the aftermeal and its proper dissemination, we can also make a very large dent in our own individual carbon footprint, If we insist on businesses recycling plastics, paper, etc., we further enable the earth to provide us its life-giving forces. So as we can see from above info, the value of the aftermeal in homes and businesses is almost equal to the total GDP of the United States. What we throw away has more value than the total GDP of 50 percent of the world's other nations. Each and every time we eat, we create a miniature garbage pile containing plastic, tin, paper, and many other items of prepackaging. If looked at in total, we have the makings of a vast fortune in trash prior to its becoming garbage.

So we wonder how do we get there, how do we grasp the gold ring of garbage? We disallow its creation. How do we disallow its creation? We separate the combination of liquids and other types of waste. Why? Because liquids are a classification of elements that provide a medium that acts as solvents for other elements to use to unnaturally combine or mix, inadvertently creating other unknown substances, usually substances that are harmful to people and other organic lifeforms. We as a society must immediately develop waste-retrieval systems to accommodate liquids only. We must stop the habit of throwing liquids into same collection canisters with dry trash in them as most dry trash can be recycled.

The government cannot handle this problem in the least as they have the bureaucracy to deal with. Classifying all the types of combinations of liquids that can accrue on a daily basis is too daunting a task. But to not allow its creation in the first place is the answer. To prevent creating of this great lake of toxic waste in the first place is the answer. To stop mixing liquids and solid waste is the key. To provide more liquid-friendly waste-retrieval systems is the single most effective way to accomplish this task present.

The Third-World Connection

Recently having visited places like the Philippines and Panama, we found their problem of toxic waste has far-reaching problems greater than we do here in the United States. Here in the United States. we have a sewer system in place with many types of landfills in place, with the ability to create more and maintain the same. The ecosystem of Islands are so complex and sometimes too small to provide space for landfills. The underground water flows and currents are an unknown entity on an Island. So they suffer a greater pain, as water-borne insects and aquatic life that start off in water suffer tremendously. As these third-world countries don't even have the waste management truck facility to even pick up the garbage bags that have filled up with toxic waste liquids in them. So it is imperative that this message gets echoed over and over to educate the world of this problem. We found them the stewards of the rain forest to be very concerned about its effects on the habitat there in the forest. We were informed that in the Panamanian jungle there still exists at least seven indigenous tribes who depend upon the forest and the bounty that it shares with them for their existence. Which is of an organic balance, yet still the ramification of garbage can be felt.

Most of the creatures of the Panamanian rain forest need and depend upon fresh water, which gathers in streams and pond to be just that, fresh and clean. The rain forest is one of the first to feel the effects of such problems as provided by toxic liquids. Most other nations follow the example as set by the United States, so the sooner we start to develop systems to handle liquid waste, the better the world will be. Oftentimes in places where there's little regulations, people often use the ocean as a place to dispose of all types of waste.

CHAPTER 3

The Solution

Who, Why, What, When: WRC (Water Reclamation Canister)

The recycling industry will continue to reward us if we simply develop a system and habits that facilitate them; by separating trash prior to becoming garbage, we will be assisting various recycling facilities to thrive.

The aftermeal, this is our mission. This is our passion. The realization of bad habits, the simplest of things can destroy or save the world. We at OMT are out to change the very way you think about trash, with a focus on the aftermeal, waste creation, and dissemination, thusly recycling.

This is why we created the water reclamation canister. It is an interactive water reclamation system (i.e., a liquid trash can). The very first step in preventing trash from becoming poisonous toxins or garbage. We recognize that the mixing of water in the form of ice, liquids with paper, animal and vegetable waste products causes poisonous toxins, liquids, and garbage to accumulate in the bottom of most black liner bags. Because modern waste retrieval collection systems do not provide a proper liquid receptor mechanism to deal with liquids, until now because liquids are the heaviest element in the bag. This makes the WRC the most important invention since the ice cube.

We include the WRC inside the waste management center as a unit to handle ice collection as it entices the user to empty their cup into the WRC prior to placing the cup in the proper container, so as to be stacked inside of one another until the cup bin is full then emptied. Cups usually come in boxes of five hundred, each usually only taking up 2 × 2 × 2' of space, but once you take twenty-five of those cups and fill them with ice, a lid, and a straw, you will have to empty the bag over twenty times to get rid of all those cups.

The waste management center can cut that amount of time you would need to take out the garbage by 80 percent. This would equate to 32 lb. of water per black liner bag. Multiply that times twenty-five bags; this equates to 800 lb. of water that would have been manually carried from inside the building to the outside waste facility. Yes, the majority of weight in garbage is water

The waste management center can reduce the number of times the black liner bag has to be emptied by tenfold, as without the addition of water in the form of ice, which adds 80 percent of the weight of the black liner bag; cups take up 60 percent of space in black liner bags. This equates to 80 percent reduction of the times needed to remove or empty the black liner bag. This is a great savings to the business owner. Plus a reduction in water bill and water usage, plus reducing each restaurant's creation of poisonous toxins, which winds up in our ponds, lakes, rivers, and streams. This product is a triple win for all concerned.

Water is widely understood to be one of the basic elements for all our survival needs. We use water for a wide range of things, not just drinking and cooking. Many of those are necessary for survival as well.

Specifically, the highest additional priorities for water are washroom facilities, cleaning, and growing plants. I'm talking about plants you are growing to eat—a vegetable garden, as well as office or business landscape. You don't need purified water for that. In reality, you'll actually use a lot more water for bathroom facilities, cleaning, and watering your garden than for drinking and cooking. That is unless you're in a restaurant-type business.

But restaurants by law have to provide free drinking water, restroom facilities, plus a nonstop supply of fresh water for a variety of other needs. So water management should be a major part of most businesses' long-term survival plan.

What Is Gray Water, and How Does It Fit In?

Once you open your water tap or faucet, all water that goes down the drain—whether you touch, use, or otherwise let it go straight down the drain—is considered "gray water," or potable water. Ice would be considered gray water. Even if never used by anyone, the fact that it has been let out of the faucet tap determines that it is gray water. So each time a patron sits to eat and does not touch the glass of water presented for that meal, that cup of water must be emptied out and a fresh cup of water must be drawn for the new patron. The term *gray water* has various definitions but is typically used to describe water that has flowed through a plumbing system that has not come into contact with feces during its journey. It can come from a sink, bathtub, or washing machine.

Used water can be broken down into two separate categories:

- *Black water.* This is sewage from the toilet. It can't be used for anything else but must go into a septic tank or sewage system.
- *Gray water.* This is water that has been used for cleaning. While it isn't clean enough for drinking, it can be used for other purposes.

The vast majority of the water we use in restaurants actually goes down the drain as gray water, not black water. This means we're essentially wasting that water.

What Can We Do With This Gray Water?

There are a myriad of ways in which gray water can be used. One last use for this water, if you can't find anything else to do with it, is use it to flush your toilets. Water that goes down the toilet can't be used for anything else, and it really doesn't need to be clean.

Making It Possible to Use Gray Water

The biggest problem most of us have with reusing gray water is that our homes are not designed for it. Every bit of water we use is flushed down drains, either into septic tanks or into city sewer systems. This is wasteful, both on an everyday basis and especially in a survival situation.

Ideally, you would want your gray water to empty into a tank where it can be reused again. It has a bad reputation, tainted by misinformation.

In "Overview of Greywater Reuse: The Potential of Greywater Systems to Aid Sustainable Water Management" (PDF), Lucy Allen, Juliet Christian-Smith, and Meena Palaniappan explain that the definition also varies around the world.

Most advocates of gray water use in the United States are championing home use in laundry-to-landscape irrigation systems, where fruit trees or ornamental landscape can be irrigated. One challenge is that its use varies by state, and some lawmakers require use permits.

The Future of Gray Water Use Is Ice

Ice is fresh water only in solid form. We use it for many purposes. Totality of the $676b drink industry use ice to condition and prepare our drinks. Which must accompany each meal that we consume at least three times on the daily. So diverting this stream of water from daily garbage collection system, will not only ease the backs of our service personnel but facilitate regenerating the recycling industry. They cannot handle or deal with raw materials that are contaminated with hazardous toxic liquids. We would be doing ourselves a great favor by simply taking three seconds more when we finish eating to throw away our aftermeal leftover in the proper receptor, if we have them there!

We are now in the future of efficient water use and savings. The liquid-waste retrieval system up until now has been absent without leave; it has been handicapped by the black liner bag. We are way past the time to deal with liquid waste effectively other than placing everything into the black liner bag.

Waste management systems are presently becoming mandatory by laws for most businesses that deal in the food service industry, because its waste usually contains animal and/or vegetable waste. Once we add water or liquids to the mix, then we have another problem totally different.

Consider the waste-retrieval system that is incorporated by hospitals, with respect to hazardous waste. It's always bagged separately, tightly wrapped, etc.; you never see liquids mixed in with needles, no way. Same philosophy should be applied to restaurant waste retrieval systems. We, the consumer, should insist that effective waste retrieval systems be employed by our restaurants and homes with respect to the waste they put out.

Following, we will show you what we think the next revolution in recycling will look like. It is the first patented liquid water reclamation canister of its kind. We are looking into developing these types of systems to further deal with leftover gray water and potable water left at a table or from liquids concerned with the aftermeal, and simply gray-water misuse.

Now we introduce to you the WRC, or the water reclamation canister. It is an interactive water-reclamation system (i.e., liquid trash can). The very first step in preventing trash from becoming poisonous toxins or garbage. We recognize that the mixing of water in the form of ice, liquids with paper, ink, animal and vegetable waste products causes poisonous-toxins liquids and garbage to accumulate in the bottom of most black liner bags because modern waste-retrieval collection systems do not provide proper liquid receptor mechanism to deal with liquids—until now. The WRC, the most important invention since the ice cube. Yes, as stated before, the majority of weight in garbage is water.

With its attractive appearance and size, it sits just next to the normal waste bin, enticing the user to empty that cup of ice into bin 1, which separates ice from any syrup, or coffee from ice, or most drinks that might contain ice. Since nothing sticks to ice as it is in a constant state of shedding or melting, any impurities will separate and drain off, allowing the ice to be melted and reused.

The bin 2 is used for potable water or unused table water. The WRC has a universal three-fourth connector, which allows connection to other water sources that might contain usable potable water, such as the soda box, which contains ice and sodas to be precooled for customers. Other such targets would be ice-filled salad bars and other devices used to hold ice.

This is what is meant by the term *interactive*. The user has ability to control what types of waters go into the system. Service personnel will have to be educated going forward with respect to types of waters that are acceptable to recycle in the WRC. *Interactive* can describe our present-day plumbing system too, see every one of us who uses the commercial sewer system, the city water-distribution plumbing system is connected to the plumbing system, so for example, if someone went on vacation and forgot to turn off the water tap with the drain open. Lake Tahoe could drain through that open tap if left unattended. Almost any home connected to the city plumbing system could waste tons of water. That's an example of how antiquated our water-distribution system actually is. Future homes will have an allotment of water per house, perhaps a small swimming pool–size amount. Which we will have to continually monitor, filter, reuse, and reuse. The present-day system, which we call the WRC (water reclamation canister), is the precursor to that functioning system.

Ice as a Gray Water Source

On a daily basis, restaurants can and are making up to and over 3K gallons of ice per day. Ice is "fresh gray water," and it has been overlooked as a resource product since its inception when it was accidentally created as a byproduct of refrigeration; since then, its importance is overlooked and thrown away. This unique element has the ability to change states so that we might introduce ice as a solid, then it becomes a liquid into the mix of all creation; this life-giving element deserves another look.

Main water class, which the WRC is targeting, would be gray water supplied by melted ice, which is basically fresh water, and unused potable table water, which has not been drunk by the customer. Other sources of unused water would come from such utilities as an ice soda box and an ice-filled salad bar. These sources of unused fresh water is just waiting for a device such as the WRC, which would welcome these sources of fresh water supplied through the universal three-fourth connector on the rear of the WRC.

There are many sources of unused-freshwater waste in restaurants; we simply have but to use our minds and construct more devices that would interact with the WRC to pump up water to secondary holding tanks, which would allow us to flush toilet and supply our gardens with this very clean and potable melted ice water. The water reclamation canister does just that, and that is what it's designed to do. It provides an effective way to deal with unused water instances. It also enables customer and service personnel to empty that cup of ice into it, the WRC, instead of saying, "But I don't have anything else to do with the cup."

The WRC is a timely device, for with water drought or not, we still need the ability to keep liquids and solid waste separate. We still need in our society this type of liquid receptor canister. This would solve the problem in most areas of recycling and elimination of the toxic liquid problem an awful lot. besides saving on using precious water resources for downright dirty applications. This product saves you money. So it actually pays for itself.

Once we are proven right, we will be introducing America to a revolution in recycling. This product is a triple win.

1.   Provides proper receptor for liquid waste, which otherwise would end up in streams, lakes, ponds, oceans.
2.   Provides a channel to save fresh water.

3. Identifies vast fresh water resource, which was otherwise ignored and discarded as toxic liquid waste (ice).
4. Assists the trillion-billion dollar industry to get on its feet: recycling.

Good ideas are sometimes dirty and messy!

WRC (Water Reclamation Canister)

Patent-pending WRC (water reclamation canister). It is an interactive water reclamation system (i.e., liquid trash can) made by OMT. Once installed, it reduces the water bill up to 40 percent and more, decreases blight on our environment and landfills
https://omtsystems.com
In compliance to performance requirements per city ordinances 3630 Modesto, California (i.e., food-producing restaurants can no longer dispose of waste "fog" in city municipal facilities, in the sewer system).

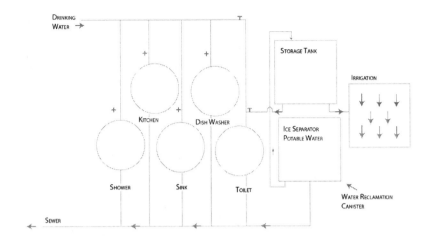

We at OMT are out to change the way you think about trash, with a focus on the aftermeal, on waste creation, and on dissemination, thusly recycling.

In the restaurant and food services areas as well as homes, the combining of liquids in waste containers, plus mixing with vegetable and animal waste, causes degeneration of paper products into toxic mess. Liquids add 70 percent of weight to garbage bags hence there is a need to separate these types of products, IE: liquids, animal and vegetable matter in trash bags less they turn into toxic garbage.

In restaurants and home applications etc, traditional waste management process is to simply place all items of waste into one generic black liner bag. Liquids and solids have always traditionally been placed in one bag. As packaging of food comprises all types of resources and material, the discharge of these materials can no longer tolerate placement in one generic bag. This usually generates toxic liquids and matter which does not facilitate recycling.

This is why we created the water reclamation canister. It is a gray-water interactive water reclamation system (i.e., liquid trash can). The very first step in preventing trash from becoming garbage. We recognize that the mixing of water in the form of ice, soda, with paper, ink, animal and vegetable waste products causes toxic liquids, which manifest itself as garbage to accumulate in the bottom of most black liner bags. Because modern waste-collection systems have not improved since the creation of the black liner bag, some ninety-plus years ago. Because modern-waste retrieval collection systems do not provide proper liquid receptor mechanism to deal with liquids or water.

Up until now, what was seen to be the greatest way to sanitarily deal with the collection of trash since modern civilization has been exposed for what it is. The largest contributor to liquid toxic waste is the black liner bag. The garbage bag. Toxic waste generators. This is what we are determined to battle against; this is why we created the WRC, (water reclamation canister). A device, a liquid utility system that will simply sit there next to the normal waste paper basket. Waiting to serve us. A place finally to put liquid waste.

A liquid canister that accepts most instances of potable water and other liquids that might contain lots of ice, which most drinks do. The aftermeal and all cleanup is usually left to the same service personnel who presented the meal. The leftover resources are once again picked up, and liquids would be picked up by service personnel who delivered same. With the possibility of such a device strategically positioned in the restaurant. The workload of having to load and unload water glasses all the way back to the kitchen can be reduced.

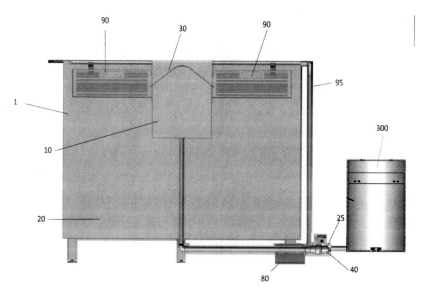

SUMMARY OF THE INVENTION

This proposed device 1 is a device and process for use with the reclaiming of water. The current invention is a gray water reclaiming container and system. It is comprised of two containers, an inner container, which captures liquids destined for drainage, and an outer liquid container for reclaiming water. There is a screen on the top of the inner container allowing ice to be filtered from liquid drinks as ice is fresh water which usually gets thrown away in cups into the trash can. The ice goes to the outer liquid container where it is melted into usable water. This usable water can be used and recycled into lawns, gardens or even used in the sanitary system to flush toilet.

There can be a filter prior to pump connected to outer container that is used to pump the recycled water out for its specific purpose of melting ice and other secondary purposes. The inner container can have drainage with a drain and run off pipe to remove the waste from the inner container for disposal. See figure 6.

The WRC is connected to a holding tank; it has filtering systems that filter melted ice and potable water, pumping it up to a holding tank, which allows water to be controlled into a landscape distribution or toilet application. The WRC can be set to recirculate onto itself in cleaning mode. The water in the holding tank will be emptied at closing time daily. No water should be retained in the holding tank for a period greater than twenty-four hours.

The holding tank can be put into a recycling mode, filtering water to remove impurities to the micro level. Holding tanks come configured in multiple sizes: 200 gal, 400 gal, 600 gal capacities. Holding tanks can be pressurized to 30 psi, which is equivalent to city water pressure, which allows it to be pumped into present-day toilet bowls and other utilities. The system can come configured to distribute into standard drip irrigation systems. Water filtered by holding tanks could be pasteurized by running through hot-water heating systems also.

The WRC is a device that melts ice. It captures the ice in the secondary filtration unit. Once melted water reaches an adjustable level in the holding tank, it is switched to overflow into the lawn application or flow into the lavatory, or into the sewer drain.

It has a primary and secondary filtration units and an ice-melting arm. Ice can be melted within a two-minute time period within the secondary filtration unit. The unit, when placed in restaurants that use over 2K of ice-making machines, will recirculate all ice placed in it; it will serve to collect unused table water and other instances of water misuse. The WRC has a three-fourth universal connector on it which avails it to other devices that might drain into it.

The WRC comes as a standalone unit or a unit in the waste management center, and can be a part of various configurations. The waste management center comes with cabinetry that would provide for various types of waste product: paper tissue goes into one bag, animal waste into another. With plastic spoons, knives, and forks into one slot with straw, lids into other. The unit can come with freezer attached and vacuum sealer attached.

Reclaimed water can be used for a variety of purposes such as environmental restoration, fish and wildlife, groundwater recharge, municipal, domestic, industrial, agricultural, power generation, or recreation. Water reclamation and reuse is an essential tool in stretching the limited water supplies in the western United States. Water reclamation and reuse research helps states, tribes, and local communities tackle water-supply challenges. Research funded under the Title XVI Program (Title XVI Research) supports the implementation of water reclamation and reuse projects under development to supplement urban and irrigation water supplies through water reuse, thereby improving efficiency, providing flexibility during water shortages, and diversifying the water supply.

Water reclamation and reuse projects provide growing communities with new sources of clean water while promoting water and energy efficiency and environmental stewardship. Water reclamation and reuse projects are an important part of Interior's implementation of the President's June 2013 Climate Action Plan and the November 1, 2013, executive order, preparing the United States for the impacts of climate change. Title XVI Research increases water-management flexibility, making our water supply more resilient and thereby helping to prepare for the impacts of climate change. For further information on WaterSMART and the Title XVI Program, please visit www.usbr.gov/WaterSMART.

Waste Management Center

The waste management center boasts of being able to reduce garbage creation and output up to 80 percent. It controls plastic knives in one chamber, spoons in one, and straws in another. These items are returned to a washing device and sterilized prior to reuse. Any damaged items are returned to the recycling industry. Specific categories of waste product can be targeted for recycling such as eggshells. This is a source of calcium; if dried and processed, this can be recycled to products that would benefit the hydroponic industry. Special shell-collector chambers are deposited at the customer's site and picked up daily, whereby collected eggshells are processed and bagged for the fertilizer industry.

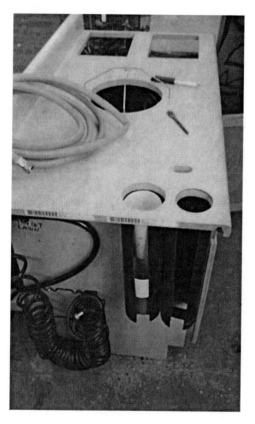

The waste management center is just what is needed: a system to facilitate effective waste management. By emptying contents of cups into the WRC, that single act prevents ice from being mixed with other stuff. The cup is stored as it was originally packaged, stacked one inside the other, in its own chamber too. This act eliminates 70 percent of space in each of the other bags, allowing us to concentrate like objects in same bag, allowing us to target various industries with their delivery. This act of sorting waste items to their respective chambers is the wave of the future. This act disallows the creation of a great amount of toxic waste creation, and considering the amount of trash that that would allow us to start recycling would be fantastic and phenomenal. This would revolutionize and spark the recycling industries. We already have infrastructure in place its getting a handle on trash, an act that is challenge. Putting in place systems and devices that would modernize the waste retrieval systems here in America. Thusly the world.

The waste management center can come with compartments that would facilitate FOG, Fats Oils Grease storage. This would comply with standards set forth in ordinance no. 3630-C.S, an ordinance amending various sections of chapter 6 of title 5 of the Modesto Municipal Code, pertaining to food-service-establishment waste water.

As described, in the future, all restaurants will be charged with tending to waste manufactured at their facility. The task is too daunting for our very own community sewer system. As population grows, arresting this problem now is more imperative. New laws as described below will assist with the speedy creation of effective waste management devices and systems. The WMC, or waste management center, can come with various configurations on it.

Laws

Ordinance no. 3630-C.S.

An ordinance amending various sections of chapter 6 of title 5 of the Modesto Municipal Code, pertaining to food-service-establishment waste management.

Some proceeds from the sale of this book will go towards development of waste-management systems that further prevention of toxic waste creation and further recycling of our water, plastic, and natural resources. The Wounded Warrior Project will also receive donations from the proceeds of sales of this book.

ABOUT THE AUTHOR

Born a Southern boy in the city of New Orleans, Louisiana, in Charity Hospital. Attended Harden Elementary School until the ripe age of nine. Lived at 2301 Tubelo Street.

I think I was a naturalist since a child. Most of my childhood memories were spent remembering the lessons my mother taught me, like every summer, instead of playing all day long, I remembered summer school lessons taught by my mother. Which I had to attend whether I wanted to or not.

Growing up, I found that these were the most important lessons of my life. The lesson of my ABCs as taught by my mother, Miss Ivy. A schoolteacher at the same elementary school. And her reputation preceded her.

My most favorite animals were birds. I had a thing for birds. I would steal all sorts of birds' eggs out of the nest if possible and try to incubate them. I got as far as keeping them alive for at least a few days in the beginning, until I figured out how to feed them.

Once, at night, I robbed some pigeon babies just hatched from an abandoned building. Took the two babies home and figured out how to feed them. I used a straw. Sucked some mixed cornmeal grits and milk up into a straw and kind of blew it into their gullets. Wonder of all, it worked, and they grew up.

They thought I was the momma. As I came home from school some days, they got very hungry if I neglected to feed them in the mornings. So as soon as I would turn the corner over a block away, they would recognize and fly to me over a block away and hover over me and, landing on my outstretched hand, implore me to feed them. All the other kids thought I was special that the birds flew to me; basically, they were hungry.

As a boy, I fished in the gator-filled swamp just over the levy, where we walked with buckets along the railroad track during the spring to pick up all the little turtles born on land trying to make it back to water. The very first thing I built was a treehouse, in the china ball tree. The china ball tree was a very important tree as we used its fruit, the china ball, as bullets to our pop guns, which we made out of abandoned hosepipe. And that's another story.

We moved from New Orleans to Chicago in 1962, south side. Graduated from Harlan High School in Chicago Illinois, 1971. Growing up in Chicago was an education in itself. One only had to live there and exist and survive to consider oneself educated in life and survival. At which time after graduation, I went back down south to Johnson C. Smith University. I got to college on a hope and prayer, and a one-thousand-dollar loan from my mother. Which got me on campus. Where I tried out for every sports team available. Landed up on the swimming team. As I won a full scholarship to swim for Johnson C. Smith University in Charlotte, North Carolina, 1971–1976.

I graduated in 1976 with a BS in PE. At which time I relocated to Chicago and started life as an adventurous young man. I tried my hand at construction work, as I entered into business opportunity with investors to start up a construction company. I left Chicago in 1979 to relocate to Minneapolis, Minnesota. In 1981, I attended Ceta CDI computer classes and began my career as a computer engineer, working on Cray Research supercomputers in Chippewa Falls, Wisconsin. That began my illustrious career as a computer engineer. Working for various Fortune 500 s/w companies.

From around 1982 until early 2013, my main source of income was derived from working with computers. I attended Master Gardener classes at UC, and in 2015, I was awakened to a world that I had been in love with since my early life as a kid on the farm in New Orleans. Since I presently own a farm, I started raising animals, like giant Flemish rabbits, guinea pigs, and worms. I started composting and loving it. Selling worms and guinea pigs and rabbits was a lesson in love of work.

The symbiotic existence between animals and plants was fruitful and rewarding. I'm presently endeavoring to try my hand at writing as I have a product that I will have to explain to lots of people I hope. As I was always motivated by things in nature, the condition of our environment has always been of concern to me. And when I'm motivated about something I usually do something about it.

So being very concerned about the water shortage I started thinking about that. This device that I have created was first done some thirty-five years ago. Yes, I was a closet activist some thirty-five years ago in my life. Back then, laws were not in my favor with respect to gray water systems. But today is a new day, and with new laws, I can see light at the end of the tunnel.

Some two years ago, I took classes at the UC Master Gardener program. I passed all class lessons with a 70 percent passing rate, but due to misunderstanding of the instructions for completing the final exam, I did not pass the final exam, as I was not allowed to retake the final exam. Still, I found the course most rewarding and fruitful as I have benefited immensely from knowledge derived from the course. That knowledge can never be taken away from me. It has awakened me to the fact that I am a natural activist as born. Knowledge has no borders.

The UC Master Gardener program is an example of an effective partnership between the University of California and passionate volunteers. In exchange for training from the university, UC Master Gardeners offer volunteer services and outreach to the general public in more than fifty California counties. Last year, 6,237 active UC Master Gardener volunteers donated 328,540 hours, and five-million-plus hours have been donated since the program's inception.

The University of California Master Gardeners preserve and encourage healthy environments with sustainable gardening practices, green waste reduction, and water conservation. UC Master Gardeners prevent, detect, and manage invasive and endemic species by educating communities about invasive species and safe alternatives. This is the UC Master Gardener's mantra.

Since it was so much in line with my own, I will adhere to its morality. Since being educated with respect to their views, I have dived back into my past only to come to the realization that being one with the universe is the way to go. Having recently remarried after being divorced after some twenty-four-plus years, I am starting to live a new life, having been reborn with a healthy respect for life and the lives of other animals that inhabit this world and my place in it.

Education:

Johnson C. Smith University, Charlotte, North Carolina (BS PE, CS)
Network Design and Administration at Sun University
CDI Minneapolis, Minnesota, Certified Computer Tech
Foothill College, Los Gatos, California (Unix and software OS)
Mission College, Santa Clara, California (programming in C)
Solaris 1x, 2x System Administration at Sun University
Veritas Volume manager training at Veritas, Mt. View, California
EMC University.
Working on VCP, VMware certified professional
Master Gardener classes at UC

CPSIA information can be obtained
at www.ICGtesting.com
Printed in the USA
FSOW01n0247060817
37162FS